Contents

Chapter 1

The Flying Saucer

The airlock door slid shut and sealed itself with a hiss. Daylight disappeared.

"We can't get out now," Dessie said. He had a habit of saying out loud things you'd like to put off thinking about. "The aliens have got us, haven't they, Zallie?"

"I expect they're friendly," I said, trying to keep him from being scared. "We won the war, so they shouldn't hurt us."

I wondered whether that sounded more convincing to Dessie than it did to me.

"Aaargh!" He fired his sonic laser gun. "Don't worry, Zallie. I'll blast them!"

That was something the war had changed. Five years ago, when it started, I was Dessie's age and I don't think I'd even seen a toy gun then. Now all the kids had them.

Well, the war was over, so why had an alien

ship landed on our farm and why had we been forced into it? Had the aliens only been pretending that they wanted to make peace?

"It doesn't make sense, Dessie," I said.

"No, Zallie," he replied solemnly, as if expecting me to go on and explain what was happening. But the only thought that was going round in my head was, *I'm responsible for Dessie and I don't know what to do*. I wished Mum or Dad were with us.

In the darkness of the alien ship, I held Dessie's hand to comfort him and thought back over what had happened that afternoon.

We were all excited because the aliens were coming to sign a peace treaty. The first ship from the Alien Federation was going to land at the spaceport to make the end of the war official.

We'd agreed to divide up space between us, and not to go into each other's sectors without asking permission first. I thought we should have sent the aliens back to their own planet, but Dad said that would have made us as bad as them.

They had spread out across the galaxy, just like us, but when we settled on a planet we fitted ourselves in so that we became a part of it. We didn't wipe out any species we didn't like, which was what the Alien Federation did. Our planet was even called Harmony.

When we'd met up with the aliens, they tried to drive us off the planets where we'd settled. Bug-eyed, barbarian monsters!

Anyway, we'd won the war and I was dying to see the Alien Federation ship land. We'd got two tickets for the observation tower at the spaceport. After all the times I'd been told I couldn't do something because of the war, I thought I deserved to go.

That was what started the argument with Mum.

"You'll have to look after Dessie," she said.

"I want to go to the spaceport." I heard my voice go whiny. "Tarrie can look after Dessie. It's his turn."

Tarrie was my older brother. He was thirteen.

"You'll be able to see everything on the holo-globe," she said, giving me a sympathetic smile to try to make me think she understood.

"I want to see the real thing."

"We can't always have what we want," Mum said more sharply. "I've got to look after the farm and someone has to mind Dessie."

The argument ended when Dad and Tarrie set off for the spaceport and I slammed out of the home-mound. If I couldn't see a real spacecraft, I didn't want to see anything.

I went up the hill behind the farm. Dessie followed me. He had to run every few paces to keep up.

"Harmony!" I muttered to myself, glancing back.

The farm buildings were almost invisible already. Our home-mound fitted harmoniously into the landscape – as did the barns and silos and storage tanks and everything. They were all built to look like small hills and were covered with grass – except for the doors and windows – so as to disturb nature as little as possible.

"Parents are mad about harmony with nature," I complained, "but they don't care about harmony with their children."

I slowed down. It wasn't fair to take it out on Dessie.

"Come on," I said, and held out my hand. "Would you like to go to the stream?"

"I'll pretend the fish are aliens," he said, waving his sonic laser gun.

The stream ran through some trees and nothing was ever touched there. Our farm bordered one of the Wild Areas which had to be left uncultivated so that the ecological balance of the planet would not be upset. The wilderness was a relief after the neatness of the farm.

We went down the other side of the hill. Dessie zoomed round me as we crossed

Lower Meadow and blasted butterflies with his gun. All it did was make this noise that first split your eardrums and then ground them to dust. Dessie loved it. Sometimes he got on my nerves.

"What do you need that for?" I asked him.

"In case the aliens come."

"The war's over," I told him. "You'll get tired of carrying it."

"I never do," Dessie said patiently, as if he was an adult reassuring a worried child. He was a strange kid.

In between zapping butterflies he talked to the cows. His "mooncows". You could see why he called them that. They had smiling, moon-shaped faces and you couldn't help being soft about them.

They were another grown-up idea of harmony. Since it wasn't allowed to bring off-world animals to Harmony in case they upset the planet's ecological balance, we'd taken some wild Harmony cattle and bred farm cows from them. Progress, grown-ups called it. I called it slavery, and said we were as bad as the Alien Federation. Dad said I was too young to understand.

The poor mooncows in Lower Meadow spent hours gazing sadly over the fence at the Wild Area. I imagined them longing to run free with their wild cousins.

Dessie mooed at them as we crossed the meadow. I don't know whether he knew what the different moos meant, but the cows always looked up and nodded their moon faces at him.

Dessie had a talent for imitating animals. His favourite joke was to creep up behind me and moo or growl. That got on my nerves as well.

While Dessie looked for fish in the stream, I lay and daydreamed about being old enough to do what I wanted instead of having to be a harmonious, mooncow daughter.

Dessie's voice suddenly cut through my daydreams.

"Zallie, what's that?"

There was something about his tone which made me sit up. Dessie didn't usually sound baffled.

I looked where he was pointing.

I don't know whether I was frightened at first or simply surprised. I'd never seen anything like it before.

"What is it?" Dessie asked again.

"I don't know," I said. "Come back here, away from it."

Hovering over the stream was a shining silver disc. It was about as big as a dinner plate and as fat as a melon. The rim seemed to be spinning round very fast. It was making a humming sound.

Also, it was watching us.

Don't ask me how I knew. It didn't have eyes that I could see, but I was certain that it was weighing us up.

"It's a flying saucer," Dessie decided, and before I could stop him he fired his gun at it.

"Stop it," I snapped.

The fat, silver disc seemed to wobble when

the noise hit it. The next thing I knew, it made a pinging sound and my leg was stinging as if a hornet had attacked me.

"Run, Dessie!" I screamed, and grabbed his hand.

Chapter 2

Captured

We ran through the trees. Or, rather, Dessie ran and I hobbled after him, one leg numb from the disc's sting.

I could hear it following us. The note of its humming rose and fell as it avoided the trees. We jinked from side to side trying to lose it. But the woods were no more than a straggle of growth on our side of the stream and in a few seconds we came out into the meadow – and stopped.

"Wow! What's that?" Dessie asked.

That's what I was asking myself.

"I don't know, Dessie," I said, giving his hand a squeeze.

In one way I did know. It was a huge, black, battered disc sitting in the middle of the meadow. It was a flying saucer as big as a barn. It was an alien spacecraft.

And it was stealing our cows.

"They're taking our mooncows," Dessie exclaimed indignantly.

"Don't do anything," I warned him.

From all round the field the cows were being herded by spinning silver discs towards the big, black flying saucer which had a ramp sloping down from a dark entrance in its underside.

The stinging in my leg was beginning to wear off.

"We're going to start walking slowly towards the gate," I said to Dessie, trying to keep my voice calm.

As soon as we moved, one of the spinning discs shot in front of us. By now I was definitely scared.

"Walk behind me," I said to Dessie, trying to keep up the reassuring tone so he wouldn't do anything sudden, though I think I was the one nearer panicking.

There was a *ping* again and I was stung on my neck. I gave a yelp. Suddenly I was angry.

I bent down, grabbed a stone and flung it at the disc, low and level, like skimming it across water.

That showed me one thing. The spinning discs were unbelievably fast. It went *ping-ping-ping*, as if it was trying to numb the stone, then it was no longer in the stone's path but hanging to one side – and all in the split second before the stone would have hit it.

"It wants us to go in the flying saucer with the mooncows," Dessie told me, sounding as calm as though everything was part of a holo-globe school programme with an interesting problem for him to work out.

I tried taking another step towards the gate. There was the *ping* and my same leg was stung again. I cried out and hobbled backwards. Either the sting was stronger this time or the remains of the last one made it worse.

The disc moved towards us and we backed away – in the direction of the flying saucer.

All over the field, cows were dancing towards it, being driven by a shrinking circle of spinning discs. We were inside the circle.

"We're trapped, Dessie," I told him.

"Be brave, Zallie," he said, as if he were child-minding me instead of the other way round.

The disc floated towards us, humming to itself like a silver insect. We continued going backwards – as helpless and stupid as the cows.

"I'm going to call them Spinners," Dessie announced, as if naming them was the most important thing we had to worry about just then.

"Stand still." I tried stepping to one side, away from Dessie. In a blink the Spinner was in front of me again, humming on a higher note.

"I think we're going to have to do what they want," I said to Dessie. "It will be less painful if we go quietly."

"We'd better get to the flying saucer first,"

Dessie said, "or the mooncows will squash us."

He had a point. Our normally peaceful cows were being driven wild by the Spinners' stings.

"Just what I was thinking," I told him. Well, I'd been about to think it. "We'd better run."

Usually you could give our cows a hug before milking, but when they got excited they seemed to grow. I didn't fancy being trampled flat in a mad barn dance.

My stings were wearing off again so we loped across the meadow, keeping a careful eye on our poor old milkers. In front of us the battered disc loomed larger and became more threatening. The airlock looked like the black entrance to a cave in a nightmare.

The Spinners stopped bothering us once we were going in the right direction, so I had time to think. We squeezed ourselves under the rim of the flying saucer, where the cows couldn't squash us. I ran my fingers across the hull. It was dented and rough, as though it had flown through a meteor shower without a force shield. I shivered. It was chilly in the saucer's shadow.

We watched the Spinners drive a cow towards the ramp. I tried to think of a brilliant idea but my brain seemed to have been paralyzed by the stings.

"Let's see if we can crawl round the other side," I suggested feebly.

We couldn't. The Spinners – or whoever had programmed them – were not that stupid. A quick look showed us that a Spinner sentry was posted each side of the saucer.

We approached one of the sentries and I could see that behind it the field on the opposite side to the ramp was clear of cows and Spinners. If I could get Dessie past, he might have a chance of escape.

"Listen, Dessie," I said. "I'll run into the open and you keep in the shadow and try to crawl round. Ready? Go!"

I ran. I held my breath the way you do when you know something's going to hurt.

The ping-sting was much stronger this time. I fell and couldn't get up for a few seconds.

Dessie was stung too. He went mad and blasted the Spinner with his gun. "I'll get you," he threatened. "If you hurt Zallie again, I'll crumple you."

We hobbled back round the saucer to the airlock. The Spinner was wobbling and humming on a different note and almost looking puzzled, as if the noise from Dessie's gun really had hit it.

"Dessie," I said quietly, "I don't see how we can get away. We're going to have to go in the flying saucer. There must be someone in there who made the Spinners. We'll go and find out who and..." I wasn't sure what next, but one thing about little kids is that they're not too worried if your plans don't end up neatly.

"Good idea, Zallie," he said, beaming at

me confidently, as if his big sister would always know what was the best thing to do.

A cow was already on the ramp. Halfway up, a curved metal bar hung over it. As the cow lurched underneath there was an electric crackle and the cow collapsed. Electrocuted. The floor of the ramp began to move and the cow was carried smoothly inside.

Dessie looked at me. He wasn't stupid.

I thought for a moment.

"What we'll do," I told him, "is follow a mooncow up the ramp and when she falls down we'll jump on top of her."

The cow we chose was poor old Andromeda. (I knew all their names.) She didn't like the idea of going in a flying saucer any more than we did. She went halfway up the ramp and came back three times. A Spinner prodded her with a sting and she bucked and kicked, but in the end she passed under the bar. There was the electric crackle and Andromeda collapsed.

"Quick," I said, and we flung ourselves on

her warm flank and rode up the ramp. The light faded behind us.

The ramp pushed Andromeda onto a metal floor which looked wet and slippy.

"Sit still until we can see properly," I said to Dessie. It was gloomy but not dark.

As our eyes adjusted we saw that we were in a big, circular metal room. The scent of animals made me think of a barn. At one end a fork-lift robot was working. It was a different shape to the ones we were used to. Alien. It was stacking the last cow on top of another animal. In the gloom I wasn't sure what the other animal was.

"That's a unicorn," Dessie said. He seemed quite pleased to have seen one at last.

"Like on your holo story-discs," I said, trying to sound casual.

The fork-lift robot reversed away from the unicorn/cow pile. It was humming to itself like the Spinners, but on a deeper note.

"Come on," I said. "We don't want to be piled up."

We climbed off Andromeda and ran to the far end of the barn – and found a triangle-shaped door. I couldn't see any way of operating it.

"Shall I knock?" I asked Dessie, as if we were visiting a friend's home-mound. I was trying to pluck up courage and keep him cheerful at the same time.

But Dessie wasn't worried about what might be behind the door. He gave it a kick. "Let us out, you aliens! We won the war!" A really tactful approach.

I shushed him desperately, but the door stayed shut, and the fork-lift robot didn't seem programmed to take any notice of our noise.

"It's cold in here," Dessie said. "Like in the big fridge in the foodstore."

"Yes," I said. My legs suddenly felt weak. I looked at the growing stack of cows. "Just like in the foodstore freezer."

"This is where the aliens keep their food," Dessie said, pleased to have fitted things into his normal world. "They eat animals."

"Yes," I said, remembering a history lesson I'd once watched on the holo-globe. It had been about the time when our ancestors had been meat-eaters. I'd never seen anything so revolting in my life. It had shown – in detail – how real, live animals had been turned into food.

I found myself imagining what a butchery robot with very simple programming might do if it confused us with mooncows or unicorns.

The last of the cows was carried up the ramp. It was Nebula. I'd fed her on a bottle when she was a calf. "Poor Nebula," I whispered to myself. I think I was really saying "Poor me".

The Spinners followed Nebula in through the airlock. The electric bar disappeared into the ceiling. There was a rack on each side of the ramp and the Spinners slotted themselves into specially shaped spaces and one by one fell silent.

As the last Spinner slid into place and ceased humming, I yelled to Dessie, "Now, run!"

But we were too late. The ramp rose swiftly to become part of the inner shell of the saucer and the airlock door slid shut. There was a hiss as it sealed itself. Daylight disappeared.

"We can't get out now," Dessie said. "The aliens have got us, haven't they, Zallie?"

That was when I had time to start wondering what was going on.

Chapter 3

The Alien

At first the darkness was like a black animal hugging our faces to its fur. I held Dessie's hand to comfort him – or myself.

Slowly I became aware that it wasn't completely dark. Patches of light began to appear on the walls. They were more like luminous blots than proper lights, but at least we could see.

The fork-lift robot was still humming but now it, too, fixed itself in a specially shaped parking bay and fell silent. Bars slid out of the walls and ceiling to make a cage round the stack of cows.

"We'd better hold on for blast-off," Dessie said eagerly.

He was right again. The aliens obviously didn't want loose cargo floating about in free-fall.

"There are slots in the wall," I said. Things were becoming clearer. "We'll sit there and hold on."

A whistling noise began. The note soared higher and higher until I couldn't hear it any more, but could still feel it going on. The whole ship began to shake.

"This doesn't feel very safe," I whispered. Why I didn't talk normally, I don't know.

"We're going up," Dessie said.

We rose, then felt ourselves tilted sideways and pressed into the angle where the wall joined the floor. As the acceleration increased, we were moulded to the shape of the angle by the crushing weight of g-forces. We were too squashed even to be able to cry out. I felt my lips being peeled back from my teeth by the pressure.

In a few minutes the acceleration decreased and we gasped for air. We'd just got our breath back when we found we had to cling on to our handholds so as not to float away.

"We're in space," I told Dessie. "There's no

gravity, so you're as light as a puff-seed."

"I feel sick."

"Swallow," I ordered. The idea of someone being sick in a gravity-less spaceship made me shrink. I could feel flying sick creeping up behind me and trickling in my ears.

I was still trying to stop imagining that when there was a huge clank.

"That was like the noise the milk tanker made when it crashed into the tractor," Dessie said.

There was more humming. This was followed by the peculiar feeling of our stomachs being pulled back into their proper places.

"I think," I said to Dessie, "we've docked with the mother ship and we've got gravity again."

"I'm cold," he said.

I'd been too worried about other things to think about that. We were in a foodstore freezer and if we didn't escape to somewhere warmer we'd soon be as stiff as Andromeda and Nebula.

"Perhaps someone will come and we can explain that we're not cows..."

"Or unicorns," Dessie put in.

"Or unicorns," I added, to keep him happy, "and we'll be taken home."

Right on cue the triangular door sighed and slid open. An alien came in.

That was when I began to feel properly sick with worry.

It was a different kind of alien.

On the holo-globe news, I'd seen the aliens we'd had the war with and it wasn't anything like them. Nor was it like any others I'd ever seen pictures of.

As soon as it appeared in the doorway, all hope of explaining anything vanished. He, she or it was a giant pear, with skin like wrinkled plastic, and a trunk coming out of the top where the stem should have been. The end of the trunk was trumpet-shaped and out of it came hooting noises.

It had two patches of waving tentacles,

like the weeds in our stream, about halfway down its front. It had four stumpy legs which it used in such a way that it glided along as if it was on wheels. It didn't seem to have eyes or mouth, and it was twice as tall as I was.

We watched silently as it drifted over to the pile of cows (plus unicorn) and hooted at them. The bars went back into the walls and ceiling. Then the alien turned and started hooting its way back to the door. At that moment my foot, which I'd had resting in a slot in the wall, slipped and thumped on the metal floor.

The alien turned and hooted madly at the wall, sweeping its trunk along towards us.

"Down," I hissed to Dessie.

We flattened ourselves against the freezing metal, as if g-forces were squashing us again. I don't know what instinct made me do that, but it probably saved our lives. The hoots passed above us and the alien glided on to the door. It hooted at it twice and the door slid open. It hooted once the other side and the door closed again.

We both let out our breath.

"What d'you think of that?" I asked Dessie.

"I'm going to call it a Hooter," he announced.

That seemed to make the alien about as frightening as a duck.

"Good idea," I agreed. "But we're still stuck in this freezer and I'm getting cold."

I had an idea of burying us among the mooncows. There would be some body heat left in their carcasses, but that wouldn't last long. I had an even wilder idea of skinning one and wrapping us in the hide. But that would take too long and, anyway, we didn't have a knife. In other words, I didn't know what to do.

Dessie walked up to the door. He hooted at it. He had to hoot three times before he got the note exact. The door slid open.

I immediately forgot about ever being irritated by his animal imitations. He could creep up behind me and growl anytime he liked.

"Let's go," I said, and we passed through the Hooter-shaped door into the main ship.

Chapter 4

The Dark Ship

We walked into a warm corridor. It was just as gloomy as the foodstore. There were luminous patches on the walls again, but they were scattered any old where, not neatly spaced out like lights.

I examined a patch. It seemed to be fungus – a luminous fungus. Clever idea for lighting a ship, I thought. Doesn't need much power.

"Hooters don't need much light to see by," I explained to Dessie, so that he'd not be frightened by the gloom.

"Are the Hooters like bats, Zallie?"

When I saw what he was getting at, it explained a few things. The Hooters found their way about by bouncing sound off objects, just the way bats did. They'd built the same guidance system into the Spinners and the fork-lift robot. That was why they hummed all the time – to see whether anything was in front of them. The Hooters made their doors operate in response to sound commands.

If you use sound to see where you're going, you don't need lights. Smart kid, Dessie. But I didn't want him getting big-headed so I just said, "That's right. You've got the idea."

I guessed that the luminous fungus was a parasite that had got into the ship by accident and the Hooters didn't even know it was there. Lucky for us. It was gloomy enough, but imagine being in a pitch black ship.

We could hear the sound of a machine along the corridor. "Let's go exploring," I suggested. We automatically went in the direction of the noise.

There seemed to be more fungus where the walls were dampest. In places, condensation ran down the rough metal. It was like being in a disused storage tank.

We came to a triangular archway and the sound of the throbbing machine made the floor vibrate.

"It's a kitchen," Dessie exclaimed.

There was a giant mincing machine taking up most of the space. Its dome-shaped lid was tipped back so that the next load could be fed in. At that moment the next load came clanking along, swinging on a hook beneath an overhead rail. It was a unicorn.

I decided we didn't want to watch what happened next.

"Do you know what a vegetarian is?" I asked Dessie.

"A sort of alien?"

"No. It's us. We're vegetarians because we don't eat animals."

We went on cautiously along the corridor. There were no Hooters about that we could see, and the kitchen had been automated, but I wasn't taking any chances.

The corridor was wide enough for two pear-shaped Hooters to pass, so it was plenty big enough for us to walk side by side holding hands. Which is what we did. So that Dessie wouldn't be scared.

"Dining-room next," he said, in the same interested voice he used when he found a shiny pebble in the stream.

He was right, of course. What do you expect to find next to the kitchen?

We came to another triangular archway and could hear bubbling and slurping sounds. Cautiously we peered round the corner.

In the centre of the room stood a huge barrel with little pipes sticking out from it. Standing round it were lots of Hooters. They had their tentacles plugged into the pipes and were making the slurping sound we could hear. Their trunks were swaying about dreamily, and now we were close we could hear a purring coming from them, like contented cats.

The bubbling sound came from a fat pipe which ran along the ceiling from the direction of the kitchen and went into the top of the barrel.

"Unicorn soup," Dessie whispered.

We spied on the Hooters for a while, then went back to the kitchen.

"I think," I told Dessie, "that we were trapped by robot hunters. It looks as if it doesn't matter what sort of animal they catch. I expect they just need protein to survive, like us."

"What's protein?"

"Well," I said, trying to remember my holo-lessons, "it's stuff to build body cells. It makes you strong. Helps your body fight illnesses and heal cuts. I think. Anyway, we all need it."

"I'm hungry," Dessie said, which got to the main problem we were facing.

I'd thought that food made from animals would smell horrible, like a dead animal in the woods, but, I'm ashamed to say, the smell of the soup made me feel hungry too.

"We'll wait until the Hooters have finished, then help ourselves," I said. "Since we're trapped in this spaceship we'll have to eat the same as the Hooters."

Dessie frowned. "Do I like unicorn soup?"

"Yes."

We counted to one thousand slowly (Dessie counted to one hundred ten times), then we sneaked back to the dining-room. The Hooters had gone.

"Let me try first," I said. "Alien soup might give us tummy ache." Or kill us with a single drop.

I put my mouth to one of the pipes and sucked as gently as I could. My eyes watered, my ears glowed and warmth flowed through my cold limbs.

I waited for any harmful side-effects. Whoever had made that holo-lesson which told you how horrible animal food was had never tasted it.

"It's all right," I said at last. While we were in the ship we'd have to eat it and try not to think about what it was made of.

We slurped like Hooters.

"Not enough salt," Dessie said when we'd finished. "I need the toilet," he added.

"Oh."

"Do aliens have toilets?"

"Yes," I said. "That's one way you can tell them from robots – if ever you're not sure."

"I expect it will be near the dining-room," Dessie said confidently.

The next room we found had nothing in it except a hole in the middle of the floor. Dessie didn't have any doubts.

"A Hooter toilet," he exclaimed. He used it.

I wondered if it really was one. It was too gloomy to see.

"What shall we do now, Zallie?"

"More exploring."

We crept further down the corridor, guided by the light from the fungus. All the walls were the same dull, damp, rusty metal.

"If you can't see," I explained to Dessie, "you don't bother to decorate your home."

"I expect they make their rooms so that their hoots bounce back beautifully," he said.

"That's what I was thinking," I told him.

Dessie had a way of making me feel *I* was five years younger than *him*.

We found more triangular archways to rooms with strange-shaped objects in them whose use we couldn't even guess at, but there were no signs of any Hooters.

"I wonder where they've gone," I said.

"Forty winks," Dessie said cheekily, "like Auntie Maccie."

I could see what he meant. Auntie Maccie was short and a bit Hooter-shaped and always fell asleep after meals.

He was right – as usual. We came to a row of archway entrances to small rooms and in each hung a Hooter in a hammock with four holes for its stumpy little legs. It swung just above the floor with its trumpet hanging down making bubbling sounds.

Dessie giggled silently. It was difficult to believe they were dangerous.

We became over-confident and went into a room to take a closer look at one of them. We should have guessed – I should have guessed –

that it had sharp hearing. It woke up and waved its trunk at us, hooting like mad.

"Stand still," I said to Dessie. "We are intelligent creatures," I tried telling it. "We mean you no harm. Please take us back to our planet."

"It doesn't understand, does it?" Dessie said sadly.

"I don't think so."

More Hooters arrived. They waved their trunks at us, as if investigating our shape by bouncing echoes off us.

"It tickles," Dessie said, squirming.

He was right. Somehow we could feel the sounds on our skin.

I tried again. "Hello. Greetings. We come in peace. We are friends. Please take us to your leader." I felt really silly saying that.

There was no response from the Hooters. They went on hooting at us and it sounded to me as though their hoots were repeating "Protein, protein" time and time again.

Suddenly they all slid back and two robots

which were Hooter-shaped appeared in the corridor. Where the Hooters had tentacles the robots had metal feelers which they waved about searching for their prey.

A Hooter trumpeted: "Hoot-hoot!" and one of the robots came towards me, its claw open.

Dessie gave a cry of rage. "I hate Hooters!" he screamed. He raised his gun – he never did get tired of carrying it – and sprayed the Hooters with brain-numbing sound.

The effect was marvellous. The Hooters reeled back in agony, waving their trumpets and clenching their tentacles.

"You don't like that, do you?" Dessie cried in triumph. "We've beaten one lot of aliens and we'll beat you too."

The robots were not affected by Dessie's gun. The first one trapped me in a corner, wrapped its feelers round me and effortlessly lifted me off the floor. The second robot did the same to Dessie.

The dreadful noise of his gun died.

Chapter 5

Prisoners in Space

....

The Hooters hooted orders to the robots and we set off in the direction of the foodstore, dangling from their feelers. I had a nasty idea what was going to happen to us. So had Dessie.

"Are we made of protein?" he asked.

"I'm afraid so," I admitted, seeing no comfort in lying: he wouldn't have believed me.

Once we'd left the Hooters behind I made my bid for freedom. I wriggled, I twisted, I drummed my feet against the plastic skin of my robot. It didn't appear to notice.

This is the end, I thought. My past life flashed in front of my eyes. All the people I'd miss: my mum and dad, my brother Tarrie, Auntie Maccie, Dessie.

"Don't worry, Zallie," Dessie said. He was

swinging quite happily in his robot's claw, as if he was enjoying the ride.

"Be brave, Dessie," I encouraged him in return.

The door to the foodstore slid open as we approached and a blast of freezing air made me shudder. I tried to think of a few farewell words to take Dessie's mind off whatever was going to happen.

But before I could come up with any, Dessie said "Hoot-hoot!" to his robot, and it opened its claw and let him go.

"Hoot-hoot!" he repeated, and mine released me.

"Dessie, you're a genius!" I cried.

Quickly we prodded the robots together.

"Hoot!" Dessie ordered. "Hoot!" The robots gripped one another with their feelers and held on.

"Well done, Dessie," I said. "I was just about to do something like that myself."

"They're dancing." Dessie laughed.

We pushed the robots and they slid easily

across the floor of the foodstore.

"Let's put them there," I said, pointing at a space between a frozen cow's legs. We wedged the pair of robots between the rigid limbs and went back to the warmth of the corridor.

"What shall we do now?" Dessie asked.

I noticed that he still had his gun. "You're not to fire that," I told him sternly, "unless I say so."

"I won't, Zallie," he promised.

"What we've got to do," I said, "is find somewhere to hide."

"I like hide-and-seek."

"Well, remember that we're protein to the Hooters so they mustn't find us, ever."

This time we went along the corridor in the opposite direction to the kitchen. There seemed to be only the one corridor in this ship. The further we went the drier the walls became and the less luminous fungus there was.

"This is a big spaceship," I told Dessie,

after I'd lost count of the number of paces we'd walked.

"We're going round," Dessie said.

"I think you're right," I agreed. "I bet this spaceship is a giant flying saucer and we're walking round the edge."

Dessie asked the obvious, intelligent question: "What's in the middle?"

"Perhaps it's the engines," I suggested, though there must have been a huge space for them.

At last we came to some more triangular archways in the wall.

"It's another kitchen," Dessie exclaimed.

It was, and that was followed by another dining-room with a barrel, next a toilet and then small rooms with hammocks. But all were empty. This part of the ship was not in use.

"Two of everything," I said. "In case the first lot go wrong."

"We could hide here," Dessie said, "and sleep in a Hooter bed."

When he said that I suddenly felt exhausted.

"Good idea, Dessie." I gave him a hug.

We climbed up into a hammock and he snuggled against me. He was asleep in seconds. I removed his sonic laser gun from my ribs and laid it on the floor.

I'd never felt so tired in my life. But I couldn't fall asleep as easily as Dessie. I lay awake and worried.

How were we to escape? We might not be locked in the foodstore but we were in a perfect prison.

Did anyone know where we were? When the Spinners captured us the whole of Harmony would have been at the spaceport or watching their holo-globes to see the Alien Federation ship arrive. We'd disappeared without anyone seeing what happened.

The next thing I knew, a Hooter had its tentacles round my throat and was trying to strangle me.

Chapter 6

Chapter 6

The Nest

I woke up struggling. My head was stuck in one of the leg holes in the hammock and Dessie was doing a Hooter imitation next to my ear. I found that he could still get on my nerves.

"You do look funny, Zallie."

"Shush! Are there any Hooters about?" I asked crossly.

"No, Zallie. I had a look in the other rooms."

I noticed that he was armed with his sonic laser gun again. I wished I had something as comforting as that to hold on to.

"I've been planning how to escape," I announced.

Dessie looked at me, his eyes shining with admiration. I felt rather guilty.

"What we've got to do is keep a watch on

the foodstore," I told him. "When the food runs out..."

"Unicorns and mooncows."

"That's right, unicorns and mooncows. Well, when the Hooters are running short of food, the Spinners will be sent down to capture some more."

"Then we'll escape." Dessie waved his gun triumphantly.

"That's the idea," I said, leaving the details rather vague since I couldn't see how we'd avoid being herded back in even if we succeeded in getting out to start with.

"You are clever, Zallie," Dessie said. I didn't argue. It was comforting for him to think so. "I'm hungry," he added.

"Me too."

We sneaked round to the dining-room. There was only one Hooter in there slurping away. It looked fatter than the others. We hid in the kitchen until it went to sleep off its meal in its hammock.

After that we fed. Cow soup or unicorn, it

all tasted the same.

"Let's explore some more," Dessie suggested, when we'd had enough.

We went past our hiding-place and on round the circuit of the outer corridor. It ran on and on. There was still no archway to let us see what was in the centre of the flying saucer. Our excitement died in the gloom.

"We must have gone nearly all the way round," I said. "We'll be back at the dining-room soon."

Dessie shook his head. "Dining-room is down there." He pointed at the metal floor.

I didn't get what he meant at first, then I understood. We weren't just going in a circle – we were spiralling upwards, and now that he'd pointed it out I saw that the curve of the corridor was becoming tighter. At some point it must end.

We plodded on, but more cautiously since as the bend became sharper a Hooter could appear more suddenly than before. The further we went the drier and darker the corridor became. I was just thinking that this was the most boring ship ever designed when the corridor ended in a triangular door. Dessie looked at me to tell him what to do.

I put my ear against the metal. There was an echoing silence.

"I can't hear anything," I said. Dessie listened and shook his head. "Do you want to try to open it?" I asked him.

Dessie hooted. The door slid open and we were hit by a wave of dazzling light and steam, just like in a kitchen.

We poked our heads through the doorway and immediately grabbed hold of it to stop ourselves falling.

"Wow," Dessie exclaimed. "It's the middle of the ship."

It was. We were at the top of a huge, flying-saucer-shaped cavern filled with pink pipes. There were millions of them, criss-crossing away below us until they became a blur. At each point where the pipes joined there was a leathery, brown lump.

"It's alive," I whispered, shivering. "Don't touch." But Dessie had reached out and squeezed a pipe.

"It feels like a mooncow's udder," he said in his interested voice.

"Don't – " I started to say, but was too late again. He poked the nearest brown lump.

It squeaked.

"There's a baby Hooter in it," Dessie said happily.

I began to think of Hooter baby-minders and warning alarms.

"Quick, Dessie. Close the door."

I took one last look at the nest of Hooter eggs. There were millions of them – enough to fill an unimaginably huge city.

Chapter 7

Escape!

....

We did not talk about the vast nest of Hooter
eggs. It was as though we had discovered
something too big to think about. But I kept
finding myself repeating, "We must escape.
We must escape." We had to warn everybody
that there was another alien race spreading
through the galaxy.

Over the days that followed, we spied on
the Hooters to learn all we could about them.
One day (I say "day" but we'd no idea of
time) we came face to face with one. Before I
could do anything, Dessie began hooting
furiously. Three hoots in a row: "Hoot-hoot-
hoot! Hoot-hoot-hoot!"

The Hooter turned quickly into an archway
and we ran past it.

"How did you do that?" I asked.

"'Hoot-hoot-hoot!' means 'Get out of the

way quickly'," he explained.

"Dessie, you're brilliant." I gave him a hug.

Every time we woke up we checked the foodstore. The supply of cows dwindled rapidly.

"When there are only ten cows left we will have to stay in the freezer," I told Dessie. "We don't know when the Spinners will be sent out hunting again and we can't risk missing our ride to freedom."

"We'll be cold."

"I've thought of that," I reassured him, pleased to be a jump ahead for once. "We'll bring the hammocks in here and make ourselves a den. We'll go in the corridor to warm up sometimes, and when we do we'll jam the door open. The foodstore won't leave if it's not sealed."

We kept checking the pile of cows.

"Our robots have escaped," I said one morning.

"Robot soup," Dessie suggested. "Unicorns

all gone as well," he added sadly.

Eventually there were only ten cows left. We moved into the foodstore – and froze. Even wrapped in all the hammocks we could find, we still shivered.

We ended up spending most of the time in the corridor. We were out there when the Hooter came. Dessie's ears were sharper than mine. He suddenly hissed: "Hooter coming!"

We ran into the foodstore. Dessie ordered the door closed and we buried ourselves under the hammocks. The Hooter came in and went hooting up to the tiny stock of mooncows. It seemed to make a quick inspection, then hooted away again, and out through the door.

"We're going down," I cried, when it left. "I'm sure we're going down."

I was right. Soon afterwards there was a clank as the foodstore was released from the main ship and became a separate flying saucer, just as when we'd first seen it. Our hammocks started to drift away from us as gravity faded.

"Quick, grab them!" I shouted to Dessie. "They'll make a cushion for landing."

We anchored ourselves against the wall and waited. As we descended we were pressed flat, but we weren't bothered about a bit of discomfort. It was the going down that mattered.

No more damp, rusty corridor. No more gloom with only luminous fungus to see by. No more cow soup. No more Hooters.

Suddenly there was a bump and everything was still.

"We've landed!" I cried. I felt like laughing and crying at the same time.

"Keep hold of a hammock," I said to Dessie.

I reckoned that as soon as we stepped outside we'd be blinded by normal daylight. Our eyes had become used to Hooter gloom. I planned to use the hammocks as shades.

"Are you ready?"

"Don't worry, Zallie," he said, as usual.

"I'll tell the Spinners to leave us alone."

There was a whirring. A blinding line of light, as piercing to our eyes as a laser beam, traced the outline of the airlock as it began to open. Then the ramp descended.

The Spinners in the rack next to the doorway started humming and rose in the air. I checked that the metal bar which had electrocuted our cows was still slotted into the ceiling.

"Come on, Zallie," Dessie said confidently, from underneath the hammock he had draped over his head.

We held hands and I guided him towards the ramp. The first Spinners flew out of the ship.

"Hoot-hoot-hoot!" Dessie trumpeted, and the silver discs obediently hummed to one side, out of our way.

We walked down the ramp and were blinded by the light. It felt like needles to my eyes even in the shadow of my hammock. I'd expected us not to be able to see, but I hadn't expected it to hurt so.

I squinted quickly in front of us. "This way." I pulled Dessie along with me. "I think there are trees over here."

Dessie wasn't even trying to see. He was completely encased in his hammock. But he kept repeating "Hoot-hoot-hoot!" and the Spinners didn't bother us.

We stumbled into the shade and stopped. I pulled the hammock tight round my head. Even then the brightness pierced my eyes. But I had to see what was happening. I forced myself to flick my lids open for a second.

"Don't open your eyes yet," I told Dessie.

"Nice fresh air," he said.

It was, but I hadn't noticed.

Open-close, open-close. Eventually I could bear to keep my eyes open long enough to focus on the ground. Brown leaf-dust.

I could hear the humming of the Spinners slowly fading into the distance.

"The Spinners must have herded all the

cows up the ramp," I said.

"Or unicorns."

I risked looking towards the flying saucer.
The Spinners were clustered round the ramp
and only one animal was left outside. It
wasn't a cow or a unicorn. I'd never seen
anything like it before.

In a way, it was like a Hooter, pear-shaped.
But instead of four stubby legs underneath, it
had two huge jumping legs. It also had two
arms where the Hooters had bunches of
tentacles, and instead of a trumpet on top it
had a pointed head.

But the most amazing thing I only
glimpsed for an instant. The animal made
one last attempt to escape, and when it
turned to face the Spinners I saw that it had a
second head right in the middle of its body.

I was still half-blind, but I'm sure that's
what it was. Then the animal turned and
bounced up the ramp like a gigantic
grasshopper.

Soup, I thought. Poor thing. Was it

intelligent like us? The Hooters wouldn't bother to ask.

I screwed up my eyes to watch the flying saucer go. The ramp and airlock closed.

"It's going," I whispered.

"Hoot-hoot-hoot!" Dessie waved his gun victoriously.

The pitted hulk rose slowly into the air. Dust billowed away from it. Through the cloud there gradually emerged a blinding yellow sun.

"Dessie," I gasped. "We're free – but where are we?"

Where was our big red sun and its little white companion? I closed my eyes in horror. I'd known we wouldn't land in our meadow again, but I'd not thought what it would be like to be marooned on another *planet*. I closed my eyes in despair.

There was the sound of a stream babbling by my ear. It was so real that for a moment I thought I must have fainted and be half-lying in water.

"Dessie!" I exclaimed.

He giggled.

I opened my eyes. I was lying on the grass between the trees and Dessie was imitating the stream, right next to my ear.

I must have fallen asleep.

It had all been a dream. No flying saucer. No Spinners. No Hooters. No—

It hadn't been like any other dream I'd ever had.

Suddenly I knew what had happened. I jumped up.

"Dessie! Quick! *Run!*"

There must have been something about my voice because he obeyed without a second's hesitation.

I ran with him. Every few bounds I glanced back to the centre of the meadow where the flying saucer had landed. There was nothing there – yet.

Chapter 8

Future-Dreams

Dessie and I ran across the meadow. His mooncows were grazing peacefully. I noticed Andromeda and Nebula. I wanted to give them a hug but couldn't risk wasting any time. Suppose the flying saucer came while I was telling them how happy I was that they hadn't after all been made into soup.

Dessie was panting along beside me.

"We can slow down when we're through the gate," I told him.

I was sure there hadn't been any Spinners outside Lower Meadow, so we should be safe there.

When we reached the top of the hill which hid our home-mound, I looked back. Everything was so normal I couldn't believe it.

We trotted easily down to the home-mound. I burst through the door, full of everything I had to tell Mum. She was standing just inside, as if waiting for me, a smug smile of greeting on her face.

"Mum," I burst out, unable to stop myself grinning like a mooncow. "I've had my first future-dream."

"Come and tell me." She smiled.

"Did you know I was going to have a future-dream?"

"I thought so. Your eye colour had gone a deeper shade."

Then I told her everything about the Spinners and the Hooters.

"It was so real," I repeated several times. "I can still feel my horror at the thought of being marooned on a planet with a single, giant yellow sun."

"Of course it felt real." Mum laughed. "It was real. You lived one possible future. You have come into your sixth sense. Any time there is danger ahead you will sense it and dream of the threat. Then you will be able to avoid it."

"What should we do?" I asked in alarm.

"We'll call up the Local Defence Centre and you can tell them exactly what you dreamed." While she was saying that, Mum keyed in the directory access codes. "Later on you will have to record your dream in detail so that all the knowledge you've gained can be stored for future use."

A head formed in the holo-globe. "My daughter has had a future-dream," Mum announced, trying not to sound proud. "An alien ship will land on — " she gave a precise map reference for Lower Meadow, "and animals will be abducted."

Then I repeated what I'd already told Mum. I had only just finished when Tarrie and Dad returned from the spaceport.

"We saw the Alien Federation ship land," Tarrie told us eagerly, not giving me a chance to say what had happened. "It was a really ugly thing."

"That's right," Dad agreed. "It was made

to fight the forces of the universe, not to flow in harmony with them."

Like the Hooters' ship, I thought. Were all aliens like that?

"It will be three days before the aliens are out of quarantine and we can see them," Tarrie said excitedly.

Dessie blasted us with his gun.

Chapter 9

Aliens From the Federation

....

The Hooters' flying saucer landed in Lower Meadow three days later. Cameras and instruments had been concealed all round the field and a wide area cordoned off for safety.

Our dairy cows had been moved and less valuable, old cows, which were no longer giving milk, had been left to graze there instead.

"Why?" I asked indignantly. "Why let the Hooters steal our animals?"

"They need food," Dad said. "You told us so yourself. It's our duty to care for travellers. We must send them on their way in peace."

"But we don't know what they plan to do. Think of all the baby Hooters in the nest."

"You're quite right," Dad replied. "We don't know what they plan to do. So, until we know for certain that they will cause harm, we must assume that they will do good and care for the universe as we do."

I could see that I had a lot to learn about harmony. I was still thinking selfishly – putting our species first.

But the flying-saucer foodstore took more than our poor, old mooncows back to the main ship. While the ramp was down, spy-robots entered it and a transmitter was attached to the hull so that we could learn more about the Hooters and plot their course through the galaxy. Someday perhaps we would make contact.

My family and I, like almost everyone else on Harmony, I guessed, were glued to the holo-globe in our home-mound. We saw the Spinners herd the animals up the ramp and we saw them electrocuted as they passed under the metal bar. It was very difficult to remember that Dessie had never seen any of this before.

"Of course!" I exclaimed. "Dessie should be an interpreter, between us and aliens.

Interpreting is the most important job there is, with so many different creatures in the universe."

"Now you're thinking harmoniously," Mum said.

It was a day for aliens on the holo-globe. After the Spinners came holograms of the aliens from the Alien Federation against whom we'd fought the war. They had spent their three days in quarantine, while checks were made, and been declared disease-free. Now they stepped onto our planet for the first time. There were six of them.

They were twice as tall as us. They walked on two legs but seemed quite steady, even though they looked odd being balanced so awkwardly.

They were like us in having two arms, one mouth, one nose with two nostrils, two ears and two eyes. The funniest thing about them was that they had no fur or hair except on top of their heads and had to cover themselves in plastic to keep warm. They were different colours, too, ranging from pink to brown.

Dessie laughed helplessly at the sight. I looked at him fondly. He was so beautiful with his short blue fur covering his four little legs which were tucked neatly under him while he watched. His body rose straight and proud above his front legs and his whiskers twitched alertly.

"Why was there a war?" I asked our mother.

"The aliens do not have future-dreams," she sighed.

"So we always knew what they were going to do," I said, "but they didn't know what we'd do?"

"That's right. They could never have won."

"Poor things," I said, looking at them in the holo-globe. They seemed to peer forward, frowning, as if they found the light on our planet rather dull. "Where do they come from?"

"Originally they came from a planet with

one large, yellow sun."

"That's where the Hooters are going!" I exclaimed. "Are we going to warn them?"

Mum shook her head. "We thought it better not to. They would probably only start a war."

"But why?"

"Creatures without future-dreams always do."

MORE WALKER PAPERBACKS
For You to Enjoy

☐ 0-7445-6977-X *Star Quest:*
Voyage to the Greylon Galaxy
by Alan Durant   £3.99

☐ 0-7445-5417-9 *Meet Me by the Steelmen*
by Theresa Tomlinson   £3.99

☐ 0-7445-6900-1 *Jeremy Brown on Mars*
by Simon Cheshire   £3.99

☐ 0-7445-6025-X *Seven Weird Days at Number 31*
by Judy Allen   £3.99

☐ 0-7445-6958-3 *The Snow Door*
by Charles Ashton   £3.99

☐ 0-7445-5277-X *The Magic Skateboard*
by Enid Richemont   £3.99

☐ 0-7445-7815-9 *Dear Poltergeist*
by Linda Hoy   £3.99

Name _____

Address _____

_____

Dyan Sheldon is a children's writer, adult novelist, humourist and cat-lover. Her children's titles include *The Whales' Song* and, for Walker Books, *Sky Watching*, *A Night to Remember*, *Elena the Frog*, and three stories about an alien cat and his human minder, Harry and Chicken.

Sue Heap has illustrated a number of children's books, including all three Harry and Chicken stories, *Elena the Frog*, *Tillie McGillie's Fantastical Chair*, and the picture books *Mouse Party*, *Little Chicken Chicken* and *Town Parrot*.

HARRY
and
CHICKEN

Dyan Sheldon

Illustrations by
Sue Heap

WALKER BOOKS
AND SUBSIDIARIES
LONDON · BOSTON · SYDNEY

For Harpo, Mao and Elvis

First published 1990 by Walker Books Ltd
87 Vauxhall Walk, London SE11 5HJ

This edition published 1997

2 4 6 8 10 9 7 5 3 1

Text © 1990 Dyan Sheldon
Illustrations © 1990 Sue Heap
Cover illustration © 1997 Sue Heap

Printed in Great Britain

British Library Cataloguing in Publication Data
A catalogue record for this book is
available from the British Library.

ISBN 0-7445-5290-7

J109, 403

£3.99

CONTENTS